Baby Bumblebee

I'm bringing home a baby bumblebee.
Won't my mommy be so proud of me?
I'm bringing home a baby bumblebee.
OUCH! It stung me!

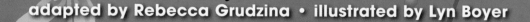

adapted by Rebecca Grudzina • illustrated by Lyn Boyer

Susie was in the park.

"I must go home now," she said.

Susie was on a street.
She saw a bumblebee.

Susie said, "This bee is a baby. I will bring it home to Mommy."

Susie was at a store.
"Look at my bee!"
she said.

"That bee can
sting you," said
the woman.

Susie was near her home.
"Look at my bee!"
she said.

"That bee can sting you,"
said the man.

Susie was home.
"Look at my bee,
Mommy!" she said.

Mommy said,
"That bee can
sting you."

"My bee is a baby,"
said Susie.

Susie was on the porch.

Susie said, "Ouch.
My baby bee stung me!"